Something Very Sad Happened

A Toddler's Guide to Understanding Death

by Bonnie Zucker, PsyD

illustrated by Kim Fleming

MAGINATION PRESS • WASHINGTON, DC

American Psychological Association

for Isaac—Your love is a constant light in my life.
I wish I'd had this book to read to you back then—BZ

for Kristy and John, and for all those who have lost
someone close to them much too early—KF

Published by
M A G I N A T I O N P R E S S ®
An Educational Publishing Foundation Book
American Psychological Association
750 First Street NE
Washington, DC 20002

Magination Press is a registered trademark of the American
Psychological Association.

For more information about our books, including a complete catalog,
please write to us, call 1-800-374-2721, or visit our website at
www.apa.org/pubs/magination.

Book design by Susan K. White
Printed by Phoenix Color Corporation, Hagerstown, MD

Library of Congress Cataloging-in-Publication Data
Names: Zucker, Bonnie, 1974– author. | Fleming, Kim, illustrator.
Title: Something very sad happened : a toddler's guide to understanding
death / by Bonnie Zucker, PsyD ; illustrated by Kim Fleming.
Description: Washington, DC : Magination Press, [2016]
Identifiers: LCCN 2016005290 | ISBN 9781433822667 (hardcover)
ISBN 1433822660 (hardcover)
Subjects: LCSH: Death—Juvenile literature. | Grief—Juvenile literature.
Classification: LCC HQ1073.3 .Z83 2016 | DDC 155.9/37—dc23 LC
record available at http://lccn.loc.gov/2016005290

Manufactured in the United States of America
10 9 8 7

Dear Reader,

First, let me express my condolences for your loss. My son, Isaac, was two years old (twenty-six months to be exact) when my mother died suddenly. Although he was fully aware of this event and tried his best to understand, he still had trouble processing the loss. After we explained, "Grandma's body stopped working," he even commented, "She just needs new batteries."

I had trouble knowing what to say when he asked questions, particularly given that I was in shock and grieving this horrible, unexpected loss. When parents are suffering and their children are suffering, it is a dual process.

As I was in the habit of reading to him every day, I searched for a book that would help him—and help me know how to best help him—process this terrible event. However, there were no books written for his age group. I found great ones that were for children ages four and up, and wonderful ones for six- to ten-year-olds, but none that were geared for the developmental age of two or three.

So, I wrote this book for two- and three-year-old children. I assure you that by helping your child understand and work through their grief, you will not only excel in your parenting role, but be better able to focus on your own grieving, as well.

Best wishes,

Dr. Bonnie Zucker

Acknowledgments

Thank you to the people who held me: Brian, Emily, Rudy Bauer, Ilene, Norm, Lisa, Sandy and Barbara Kaye, Mary Alvord, Bernie Vittone, and Robert Footer. Thank you endlessly to Sarah Fell and Kristine Enderle for making this book happen.

How to Use This Book

This story is intended for you to read to your two- to three-year-old child. It can also be used as a starting point for children a little older, but they may benefit from more information than that which is provided here.

Since the two- to three-year-old child cannot read, you can personalize the story by using the name of the loved one who died, and the correct pronouns. You will find that certain words are color-coded in red to cue to you to substitute with the person who died ("Grandpa," "Daddy," or "Mommy", for example) and to change the pronouns from "she" to "he" and "her" to "him," when appropriate. Though subtle, this distinction is really useful for children, as it will help them understand better. You may wish to read it yourself first, before reading it to your child, to help you have the flow when reading it to your child. It is best to read this story as soon as possible after the death occurs. Try to find a quiet space to read the story to your child, and allow time to help your child process the story and drawings, and answer questions. I recommend reading it during the day, not as a bedtime story. Introduce the story by saying something like, "I have a special story to read to you. It's about Grandma." I would not push reading it. If your child is not focused or uninterested, say, "No problem. I'll leave it here and we can read it later."

Something very sad happened.
Grandma died.

When someone dies, their body stops working.
Grandma's body stopped working.

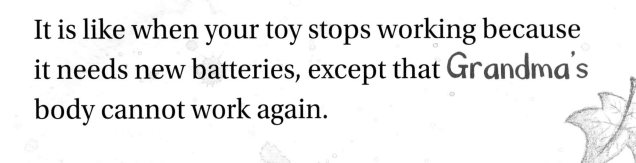

It is like when your toy stops working because it needs new batteries, except that Grandma's body cannot work again.

It's okay to feel sad or scared,
and it's okay to cry.
Mommy may cry, too.

It's okay to feel mad.
Mommy may feel mad, too.

If Mommy
cries,
it's because
she feels sad.

Because she misses Grandma.

When someone dies,
you cannot see them anymore.

We cannot see
Grandma anymore.
That's why we will
miss her.

When someone dies,
you cannot talk to them anymore.
We cannot talk to Grandma anymore.
That's why we will feel sad.

But we can look at pictures of her and
we can tell stories about her.

You can still love her,
and she will always love you.

Love cannot die.

Note to Parents and Caregivers

The following sections provide guidance on how to handle dealing with the details of the loss with your two- to three-year-old child. This is a sensitive and challenging time for you and your child and being prepared for how to talk about death, answer questions, and maintain your connection throughout the process will benefit you both. It is normal for your confidence to fluctuate during this time, but the more you know about how to guide your child through it, in an atmosphere of openness and nurturance, the stronger you will feel in your ability to help them navigate the loss.

General Tips for Helping Your Grieving Child

It is essential to know how to relate to your child's developmental understanding of death, and to have realistic expectations of their capacity at this age. This will allow you to see their reactions as normal.

- Children at this age are aware of death, even if they cannot comprehend what death is. They are also aware of what is going on in their environment.
- Be authentic and honest, as much as possible; acknowledge that you and everyone around the child are sad, and explain why. It is not healthy to deny that someone has died, or that something bad has happened. It is very important to help your child make sense of what is going on around them.
- Children at this age do not understand the irreversibility of death, and therefore will likely believe that the person can come back, or that they will see the person again; this is normal and the child will eventually understand the permanency of death.
- It is normal for children at this age to repeat what they have been told about the person dying. This repetition may be hard for you to hear, but it is how the child processes the information.

- In general, the more you talk about the loss, the better. The more comfortable you are talking about it, the easier it will be for your child to process it. Acknowledge that everyone is sad.
- As much as possible, try to keep the same routine for the child. The fewer disruptions, the better, particularly around bedtime rituals. Don't introduce big changes like potty training or moving out of a crib shortly after the loss.
- Your child may regress to earlier behavior or be very clingy with you; this is a normal expression of grief in a child this age, and does not need to be addressed directly. Rather, put your efforts into helping your child process the loss.

Talking to Your Child About Death

Choosing the right language to use with your child allows them to properly understand and grasp what has happened. Be thoughtful and intentional about the specific words you use.

- Use concrete, simple, and straightforward language (like the language used in this book), and avoid euphemisms such as "passed away," "resting in peace," and "it's like a long sleep." These euphemisms confuse children and make it challenging to grasp what has happened.
- Provide an honest explanation of death and repeat it frequently. For example, "His body stopped working so he died. When someone dies, they cannot eat, sleep, or breathe anymore," or "He was very old and his body stopped working. He died." It may be hard for you to say these words, but this language is necessary for the child's understanding.
- Depending on your values or beliefs, you may decide to explain the concept of heaven or an afterlife. For example, you may say something like, "Grandma's body stopped working and she went to heaven. Heaven is a place we cannot see and it's where you go when you die. It's hard to understand, but you don't take your body to heaven. She can send her love to us,

and we can send our love to her, but we can't see her or hear her." Avoid saying "Grandma is in heaven now and she's happy and at peace," because your child may be confused about this (why would Grandma be happy when we are all sad?).

- Keep in mind that if you are going to tell your child that the loved one went to heaven, or is in heaven now, that this means you cannot use the term "heaven" to describe wonderful daily events. (For example, I told my son that my mother "is in heaven now" and when a Whole Foods opened up near our home, I walked in with him for the first time and commented, "Wow, this place is heaven!" He replied, "Grandma is here?"). You may also have to correct those around you as well, gently explaining that the child will be confused by other references to the term.
- If your child expresses fears that they might die or be sent to heaven, provide direct reassurance: "You are okay and you are not going to die. You won't go to heaven for a long, long, long, long, long, long time. Your body is strong." At this age, providing reassurance is necessary in response to personalized fears that this could happen to them; however, for older children, repeated reassurance like this could potentially strengthen death anxiety.
- Create space to be with your child, make the time to connect with them and give them space to process whatever they are experiencing.
- Provide physical comfort and connection.
- Reassure your child that they will be taken care of, and that it will be okay.

Answering Your Child's Questions

Your child will rely on you to answer their questions. Questions may come up spontaneously or randomly, or during a time when you are discussing the loss; regardless of when, it is most important that your child's questions are answered at the time they come up. It can be hard for you to repeat the answers, but your child will often require repetition.

- Encourage your child's questions and make sure your child understands what you are explaining. Ask once or twice (not repeatedly), "Do you understand what happened?" and "Do you have any questions?" Let your child take the lead in asking questions.
- Your child's reaction may be surprising at times. Months from now, they may suddenly talk about the loss. Whenever they bring it up, communicate the same openness and willingness to listen and discuss further. It is normal for the loss to be revisited and your goal is to further your child's understanding by answering their questions, even when they are repetitive.
- Your child may feel abandoned by the loved one. Reassure your child that the loved one is always going to love them and that love never dies.
- Your child may believe that the person will come back, or is still doing the normal things they did but just doing them somewhere else (e.g., eating dinner in heaven). If they ask, re-explain: "Grandma's body stopped working so she died and we can't see her anymore." Or, "Her body doesn't work anymore, so she can't eat anymore. She doesn't have to eat now."
- Children may express concern about who will feed or bathe them or put them to bed, and it's important to provide answers to these questions and reassurance.

Being Emotionally Available and Modeling Healthy Grieving

Your child is not the only one grieving. Many people try to hide their grief in efforts to shield the child, but then they miss the chance to model what is normal and appropriate when a loved one has died.

- You can model appropriate grieving to your child; this means that you can show your child by example what it means to grieve in a healthy way. You can normalize feeling sad and explain to your child that this is what happens when someone dies.
- Hiding how you feel may confuse your child.

In addition, children can often pick up on nonverbal cues and may misunderstand why you seem different to them.

- Be honest and authentic: when you are upset or crying, say, "I'm feeling sad. I miss Grandma."
- When you cry in front of your child, reassure them: "It's okay. I'm okay."
- If you are struggling with uncontrollable crying, it's best to take a moment by yourself as this may make your child feel scared.
- Even when you are crying, you can hug your child and when your child hugs you back, say, "I feel sad but hugging you makes me feel better." This teaches the child that physical affection can make them feel comforted and safe, and also helps them grow into a loving person.
- Model how you commemorate the person who died. Carry a photo with you, or wear something that belonged to them. For example, I wear a ring that my mother wore daily and my son knows "that was Grandma's ring," and that it helps me feel close to her. Again, explaining these concepts will help your child process the loss and grieve effectively.

Dealing With Your Own Emotions

You can only do your best in life, and your best will vary based on different circumstances. When grieving, you need to be realistic about what "best" is and be gentle with yourself and your child.

- Be compassionate with yourself when you have a bad day. As obvious as this is, some days will be harder than others and you need to be compassionate and kind with yourself on the days when you are not at your best. There will be periods of equilibrium and disequilibrium.
- Take time every day for yourself, time when you can be without your child(ren) and can focus on your own sadness. Even fifteen minutes before bed is helpful.
- Ask for help from others. Seek support. Don't try to take care of everything on your own. Accept that some normal daily tasks won't get accomplished—chores may not get done, or

bills may be paid late. All of this is normal.
- Nurture yourself: for example, write in a journal, take baths, do restorative yoga, meditate, go for walks, or read about grieving.
- The children of adults who do their own work on the loss have a lower level of traumatic grief. Don't hesitate to get help. Individual or group therapy can benefit you. Most states have a psychological association with a referral service or you can ask your physician for a referral; www.apa.org and www.nami.org are also excellent resources.

Funerals and Cemeteries: What to Expect

Most people struggle to some extent with what to do regarding the funeral and going to the cemetery. The following is intended to guide you through the decision process.

- While I recommend that most two- and three-year-old children do not attend funerals, I always respect someone's decision to bring a child this age to the funeral (and understand that sometimes it may not be feasible not to bring them). The reactions of those present can scare the child, and the rituals (e.g., putting dirt on the coffin once in the grave) can be confusing to the child. Additionally, your child's presence can make it harder for you to be completely present at the funeral. For example, if it was your parent, spouse, or sibling who died, you need the time to be focused on the loss and process saying goodbye to your loved one; having your child there to tend to may interfere with this process.
- If you do take a two- or three-year-old to a funeral, explain the ceremony to your child in age-appropriate terms. For example, "The funeral is when we talk about Grandma and how special she was and how much we love her." It is also important to normalize your child's questions and feelings. For example, children may worry that the loved one cannot breathe if they are underground; explain that they don't need to breathe because their body stopped working. Depending on your values and beliefs, if you choose, you can also explain

that they are in heaven or the afterlife now, not in their body anymore. I would caution against having children this age at a viewing as this may induce trauma.

- I do recommend commemorating the loved one who died in an age-appropriate way (see below). For example, at the funeral, you could have the child place a flower on the coffin or grave, or you can put a picture of the child or a drawing by the child inside the coffin.

- Taking your child to the cemetery can provide a useful way to connect with both your child and the loved one you lost. Make it a very warm and loving experience for your child. For example, you may tell your child something like, "This is a special place to think about people who have died," or "We can think about Grandma here." When I take my son to the cemetery, I tell him stories about my mother, he "plants" roses and pinwheels, and we put seashells and silver hearts on her tombstone. He feels good about planting the roses and arranging the hearts; it gives him a chance to do something for her, and as you can guess, means a great deal to me.

Commemorating the Person Who Died

Commemorating the loved one can be emotionally challenging but also incredibly rewarding. This is another opportunity to guide your child through the grieving process and model healthy grieving.

- Ideally, the child should have a photo of the loved one who died (preferably one of the child and the loved one together). If this is not possible, drawing a picture with your child of the person who died would be second best.

- Make a photo album or memory book of the person who died, including pictures of the child with him or her. When my mother died, I made a photo book of all of the pictures of her with my son; at the unveiling (a year after her passing, when the gravestone is revealed in Jewish tradition), I made an audio CD of ten of her favorite songs which I also played

for my son on a regular basis. These projects also brought me great comfort. Taking action around grief is one way of moving through it.

- Watch videos of the loved one.
- Light a candle in honor of the loved one.
- Have the child make a drawing, other artwork, or even Lego creation, for the loved one.
- Have a birthday cake with candles on the birthday of the loved one who died or do something in honor of them on their birthday. Explain the significance of these activities to your child. Even though they are not with you, you can foster a connection to them through doing what they would have loved to do. For example, for my mother's birthday, I took my son to the Phillips Collection art museum in Washington DC, as my mother was an artist; on another one of her birthdays, we took a train to Baltimore which was a special adventure since my mother loved adventure and travel, and since she would have loved seeing my son so happy on the train. I shared the relevance of these activities with him at the time.
- Tell stories about the loved one.
- Bring your child to places and do activities that the loved one enjoyed.

Guidance for the Future

As you move forward, your child will likely form new thoughts and have an evolved perspective around the loss. Meeting your child where they are in the grieving process will help them feel understood and continue to support their grieving work.

- As your child gets older, they will revisit the loss with a new level of questions and a new level of awareness. Ultimately, they will understand the irreversibility of the loss. With this new awareness may come a new sadness, or a resurfacing of grief and possibly regressive behavior. The goal is to help your child process the loss again, while integrating their more sophisticated understanding of it. Two years after my mother died, my son asked me a lot of questions he didn't think to ask when he was two.

- As your child gets older, they may talk less and less and remember less about the person who died. They may forget their time with the person and may not remember what they looked like (in this case, you can show your child pictures). While this will be sad for you, remember that the love and time with the one who was lost mattered and contributed to your child's experience in life. The influence was there, though the memory of it may not be. In addition, by commemorating the loved one, you can help sustain a connection to him or her.

If your child's grief does not gradually lessen with time, seems overwhelming to them, or interferes with your child's daily activities (for example, if you notice disruptions in their sleep pattern or persistent irritability)—or if you simply wish for more guidance or support with helping your child process the loss—it is recommended that you seek help from a licensed psychologist or other licensed mental health professional. Remember that it is important to take care of yourself and process your own grief, as well. Do not hesitate to seek help if you need it.

About the Author

Bonnie Zucker, PsyD, is a licensed psychologist in private practice. She received her undergraduate degree from George Washington University, her master's degree from the University of Baltimore, and her doctoral degree from the Illinois School of Professional Psychology in Chicago.

Dr. Zucker specializes in the treatment of anxiety disorders and is the author of *Anxiety-Free Kids* and *Take Control of OCD*, and co-author of *Resilience Builder Program for Children & Adolescents* and two relaxation CDs. She lives in Bethesda, Maryland with her husband and two sons, Isaac and Todd (named after her mother, Thelma).

About the Illustrator

Kim Fleming has always been passionate about creating visual content for children. Her specialty is children's books, but her illustrations can be found in many different places, from children's games to greeting cards. She enjoys working traditionally, and creates her illustrations using watercolor, pencil, and lots of love.

About Magination Press

Magination Press is an imprint of the American Psychological Association, the largest scientific and professional organization representing psychologists in the United States and the largest association of psychologists worldwide.